The Bridge Dancers

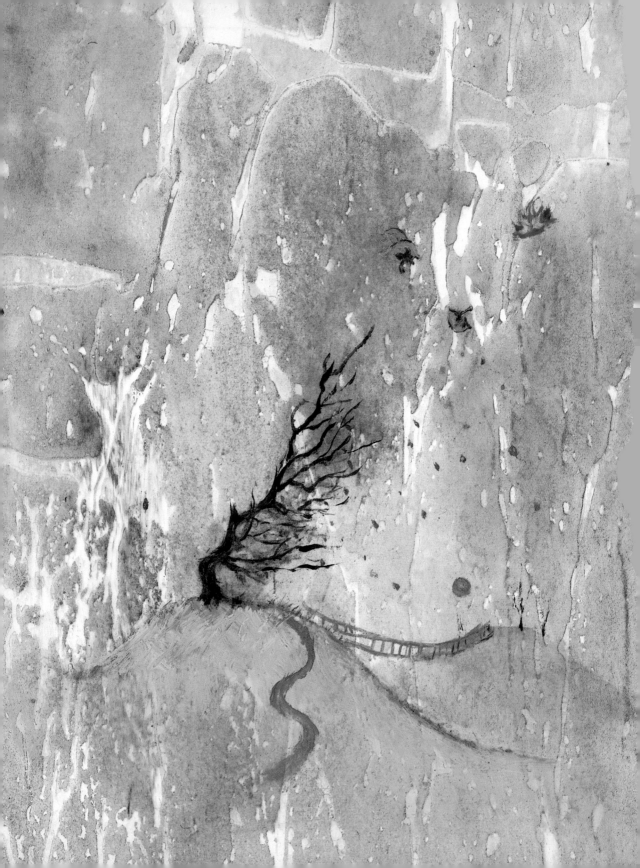

The Bridge Dancers

by CAROL SALLER

illustrated by GERALD TALIFERO

 Carolrhoda Books, Inc./Minneapolis

Mama gives the comb a yank through the mess of Callie's long, wild hair, and Callie gives a yell like you've never heard before. That's not to say *I've* never heard it before; I've heard it plenty. Callie says when she grows up she's going to the city to live, where she'll start a new style. All the ladies will come to her and pay a lot of money to get their hair tangled up in knots, and she'll get rich and never comb her hair again.

1'm not a lot like Callie. My hair doesn't fly around much, and I like it combed, and I don't often think about leaving this mountain. Callie's going to be thirteen soon. I'm only eleven, and I've never even been across the bridge.

When Callie's all combed, we go down the path to the bridge. It's our favorite place to play when our chores are done. The dirt path is steep from our house down the twisty old hill. We like to run down fast, bouncing off the little trees in a crazy zigzag, but when we reach the edge of the gorge, the path levels off and we run alongside it. To folks way down below on the river we must look like two little pokeberries, up high on the mountain's edge.

What we call the bridge isn't the real bridge, where horses and buggies can get across, that's a few miles off along the path. Our bridge is just a shaky old skeleton, a tangle of ropes and boards that ripples and swings in the breeze. Our house is the closest one to this bridge. The next nearest is the Ketchums' place, another mile up the mountain. Most of our neighbors live across the gorge; Mama says there are seven houses within the first half hour's walk. Mama often has to cross the bridge, but we're not allowed.

On this day, the wind is strong and the bridge is

rocking like a boat in a storm. We make clover chains and toss them into the gorge, watching them blow away and then down, down. We count the seconds till they hit the water far below. Callie stays by the edge, but I spy some yellow-eyed daisies growing up the hill a ways, and I know Mama will want them. If you boil daisies—stalks, leaves, and all—it makes a tea that's good for coughs, or a lotion for bruises and sores. Mama doctors most of the folks on this mountain, and we always keep a store of dried plants for medicine. I pull the best ones and put them in my apron pocket.

Later, when the sun is behind the mountain and I'm getting cold and hungry, I start back up the path, but Callie doesn't want to go. "Maisie! I dare you to stand on the bridge!" she calls, just like she does every time we're here. I don't answer, but I stop and turn to look. She knows the thought of it scares me.

Now she skips up the hill a little ways and stands on her toes like a dancer, her skirt ballooning in the wind. In the gloomy light of sundown she is ghostlike

and beautiful. "Announcing . . . Calpurnia the Great!" She twirls and leaps and strikes a pose with one toe pointed forward: "Calpurnia—the Daring Bridge Dancer!"

I laugh. I'm pretty sure she's only teasing. Callie dances toward the bridge, humming a tune that she imagines sounds like a circus. When she gets to the part of the bridge that sits on land, she holds onto one post and points her foot out toward the gorge, leaning back in a swoop. Then she glides out onto the bridge, stopping to spin slowly, arms in the air. She starts to slip, but before I can cry out, she turns back, laughing. My heart is jumping. I'm getting ready to run and pull her away from the bridge when she skips aside quick as lightning and starts chewing a piece of clover. In a second I see why.

Mama is huffing down the path. She's lugging her doctoring bag and has to watch her step. If she'd seen Callie fooling around on the bridge we'd both have caught it. "Girls, I've got to attend to Mrs. Gainie,"

Mama says, putting her bag down for a rest. "She thought the baby would come last night, but tonight's the full moon. It'll come tonight." She looks us over and frowns across the gorge. "I might be gone till sunup, so get yourselves some supper, and don't forget to bolt the door, you hear?" She points at some dark clouds moving fast across the sky. "Hurry on up. I've already made a fire—there's a storm blowing." We nod. She starts for the bridge.

"Mama?" I call, and she stops and turns. "Is Mrs. Gainie going to be all right?" Mama nods. "She's a strong woman." She reaches for the bridge rail with one hand.

"Wait!" I call.

Mama stops again. "What is it, Maisie?"

"Have you got the tansy I picked?" I ask. Tansy is supposed to help a baby come, but if it doesn't do that, at least it keeps the bugs away.

Mama says, "I've got it, but I don't expect to need it this time." She smiles at me. "I'll mind my steps on the bridge, Maisie." Mama knows I'm afraid.

When Mama crosses the bridge, I never let go of her with my eyes. She's a big, heavy woman, and when she steps off the land part, the whole bridge from one side to the other dips into a sharp V with Mama at the bottom point. She goes slow, holding the ropes with one hand and her bag with the other, and she walks in a careful rhythm, giving the bridge time to bounce just right between steps. Callie says, "She won't fall if you look away," but I never look away. On the other side it's already dark, but we can just see Mama turn and wave. We wave back, and Mama disappears around the side of the mountain down the path to the Gainies'.

"Come on, Callie," I say, starting up the path. I know that there's supper to get and more wood to gather and plenty else to do. But Callie isn't of a mind to work. She throws her blade of grass to the wind and runs ahead of me, her arms flung wide. "Burst into jubilant song!" she cries. "The everlasting chains are loosed and we are free!" Callie gets a lot of big words from reading the Bible. "Let us soar into the heavens, never to be enchained again!"

With that, she scampers off the path into the brush, and is soon just a pale flutter in the dusk, dancing and dodging among the trees. I feel the first drops of rain, and in a moment Callie is back.

"Maisie, I know what let's do," she says, blocking the path. She has to raise her voice now against the wind.

"What?" I ask with a frown. Callie's smile looks like it's hiding a bad idea, and I'm not sure I want to know.

"Let's get the ax and split a log for the fire," she says, wrapping her skirt around her and skipping along beside me. "There's a big storm coming. Let's have a fire that will last us all night."

I'm not sure. A fire would be good on a cold, stormy night, and I know there's only kindling left in the box. But Mama's the one who chops the wood. She takes down that big old ax from its pegs high on the wall and tells us to stand away. She's never told us not to touch it, but I have a feeling that we're not supposed to. I shake my head. "Callie, I don't hardly think you could even lift that ax. You're likely to get yourself killed." But my words blow away with the wind, and Callie is already halfway up to the house. I start to run, too, but I've never yet stopped Callie from doing what she wants to do. I figure the best I can do is be there when she needs help.

When I get to the door, Callie has the lantern lit and is dragging the rocking chair over to the wall. "Don't stand on that—it's too tottery!" I cry, and I run to hold the rocker while Callie climbs up and waits for the wobbling to stop. When the chair is still, she reaches up both hands to lift the ax from its pegs. It's heavy, all right; I can see by the way Callie's muscles stand out on her arms. Just when she's got it lifted off the pegs, the wind blows the door shut with a powerful "bang!" and we both jump with fright. The rocker pitches, and Callie falls.

For a long moment it seems like nothing happens. My thoughts stop; even my heart seems to stop. Then Callie is crying out with pain and fear. It's her leg, cut deep by the ax. She clutches hold of my arm, tight, and gasps with the force of the pain. "Maisie, hurry and get Mama!" she whispers. "Callie . . ." I start to say, thinking about the wind, the dark, the bridge. Callie sees how I don't want to go, and she looks at me, begging with her eyes. "Maisie, I'm sorry—but you've got to go! You're the only one who can help me!"

I don't want to think about what Callie is saying. Instead I grab one of the clean cloths Mama uses for straining her herb medicines, and with shaky fingers, tie it tight around Callie's leg. I take a quilt from the bed and put it over her, then run to the kindling pile and throw an armload of sticks on the fire. Callie is crying; the wind is crying. I light another lantern and wonder how I can cross the bridge, in the night, in the storm.

Outside, the wind and trees are whipping at the sky. I hold my skirt in one hand, the lantern in the other, and stumble in the quivery light down the path to the bridge. With my whole heart I wish there was some other way to fetch Mama. I think of Mama with her jars and packets, her sure hands and her healing ways. She'll stop the bleeding with a poultice of yarrow; she'll make an herb tea that will help Callie sleep. But Mama is far across the valley—how will I ever cross that bridge . . . Near the bottom of the hill, I can hear it before I see it, ropes groaning and boards creaking, as it tosses in the storm.

I stand at the edge of the gorge, my lantern lighting the first few steps of the rain-slicked bridge. The fear in me is so powerful it stings my eyes, and I know I don't have the courage for even the first step. But I remember what Callie said—"Maisie, you're the only one who can help me"—and I step onto the bridge with both feet.

The bridge pitches and plunges. I grab for the
ropes, and the lantern flies from my hands. "No!" I
shriek, as it rolls away and drops into the darkness.
On my hands and knees, I crawl back to the edge of
the gorge, sobbing in the terrible black night, crying
for Callie, crying for Mama. How can I cross the
bridge...how can I help Callie...think what to do,
Maisie, think what to do. With my face near the
ground, I make myself take slow breaths. I can smell
clover, damp with rain.

Suddenly, I know what to do. I pick myself up and
start back up the path, feeling my way in the darkness,
guided by the small light in the house at the top of the
hill. I remember all the times I've watched Mama
with her bag, with her poke leaves for burns, her
chickweed for tummyache. It's the yarrow plant that
stops someone bleeding, and I can make the poultice
myself. Near the top I begin to run.

When I burst in through the door, I see that
Callie's face is pale. "Maisie—Mama!" she says,

weakly. "There, Callie, don't fret; it's going to be fine," I comfort her. "I know what to do. Mama will come later, but I know just what to do."

My hands shake a little as I set the kettle on to boil—the fire is still burning strong. Then I go to Mama's cupboard of crushed and dried plants. I find some yarrow and wrap it in a clean muslin cloth to make the poultice. My fingers are sure now—Mama does it exactly so. Then I take a handful of dried feverfew and put it in a pot, for tea. Callie is moaning, so I sit by her and talk. "Yarrow is just the thing—and I remember I picked this myself! It has such pretty little flowers, and so many funny names: thousand-leaf, angel flower, bunch-a-daisies, sneezewort. It won't take but a minute, once that water's boiled. Don't you worry, Callie. Maisie can take care of you."

When the water is boiling, I pour some into the teapot with the feverfew and put it near the window to cool. Then I put the wrapped-up yarrow into the

kettle and put the kettle back on the fire—not too long, just long enough for the water to soak in and soften the yarrow. Then I scoop out the poultice with a ladle, and after a minute, while it's still hot, I put it carefully on Callie's leg. I know it will hurt, so I keep talking. "Listen to that rain! It's really starting to pour now. You know, this is a pretty bad cut, Callie, and it hasn't stopped bleeding yet. This poultice will stop it. Can you smell how sweet?" But Callie yells when the poultice touches her leg.

When the tea is cool, I pour some into a cup, and hold up Callie's head for her to drink. "That's good," I tell her. "This will ease the pain. Maybe you can sleep a little; sleep till Mama comes." I rest her head in my lap, leaning my back against the wall. Rain thrashes the roof as I stroke her hair, all tangled and wild. I talk on and on, about ox-eye daisies and Queen Anne's lace, chickweed and tansy, the names like song words, lulling her to sleep at last.

When Mama came home early the next morning, she found us sleeping on the floor. She unwrapped the cloths and washed out the cut—Callie hollered like anything—and said I'd done just what she'd have done herself. She never scolded about the ax—she knew there was no need—but she did ask why I hadn't come to fetch her. I was ashamed, telling Mama how I'd been too afraid to cross the bridge. "You've got good sense, Maisie," she answered. "I guess there's more than one way to cross a bridge."

It's been three months since Callie was hurt, and she's healed as much as she ever will. There's a fearsome

scar on her leg, but Callie says that when she goes to live in the city she'll wear long pants like the men and no one will ever know.

Ever since I took care of Callie, Mama has let me help her with the doctoring. From the time I was little, I've helped her find and dry the flowers, but now I go along and watch when she tends to sick folks. When Callie talks about the city, I sometimes think I might visit her there. But for me, I think the mountain will always be my home. I like the way the mountain needs Mama. Someday I think it's going to need me, too.

To Mom
      —C.S.

This edition of this book is available in two bindings:
Library binding by Carolrhoda Books, Inc.
Soft cover by First Avenue Editions
241 First Avenue North
Minneapolis, MN 55401

LIBRARY OF CONGRESS CATALOGING-IN-PUBLICATION DATA

Saller, Carol.
   The bridge dancers / by Carol Saller.
      p.   cm.
   Summary: When her older sister cuts her leg in an accident,
Maisie uses the knowledge of herbal medicine she learned from their
mother, a healer in their mountain community.
   ISBN 0-87614-653-1 (lib. bdg.)
   ISBN 0-87614-579-9 (pbk.)
   [1. Herbs—Therapeutic use—Fiction. 2. Folk medicine—Fiction.
3. Sisters—Fiction. 4. Mountain life—Fiction.] I. Title.
PZ7.S15325Br   1991   90-2585
                                                          CIP

Manufactured in the United States of America

      3   4   5   6   7   8   9   10   00   99   98   97   96   95   94   93